Echoes of Lost Love

(A Love That Couldn't be Healed)

Written by
Alaa Zaher

The material and intellectual ownership of this book is subject only to the author, and any modification or copying of the contents of this book without the author's approval will be considered an infringement of the author's intellectual and material rights, as well as the personalities within the book from the author's inspiration, and has no connection to reality and if it is found in reality it is a coincidence. This is a work of fiction. Similarities to real people, places, or events are entirely coincidental.

Copyright © 2024 Alaa Zaher.

Written by Alaa Zaher.

Chapter One: The Meeting

Paris, with its cobblestone streets and unending charm, was blanketed in shades of gray as the rain steadily fell, creating a rhythm on the windows of a small café by the Seine. Inside, a young artist named **Veronica** sat by the window, her sketchbook open, and her pen gliding smoothly across the page. The café was a refuge from the storm, its warm light contrasting sharply with the dreary weather outside.

Waiter: What would you like to order?

Veronica: I'd like some coffee, please.

Waiter: What kind?

Veronica: A latte would be great.

Waiter: Okay.

The **waiter** left and soon returned with **Veronica**'s order. **Veronica** loved these rainy days. The world seemed quieter, more contemplative, allowing her mind to wander freely. She often found inspiration in how people interacted with their surroundings, each moment a potential masterpiece. Today, however, her attention was drawn to a man sitting alone at a table in the corner. He was engrossed in reading an old book, his brow furrowed in concentration, and there was an air of melancholy about him that piqued her curiosity.

She watched him for a moment, noting the lines of stress etched into his face and the way his fingers absently traced the edges of the book's cover. Succumbing to her curiosity, **Veronica** began sketching the man, capturing the way the light fell on his face and how he held the book as if it were a lifeline. She often found inspiration in the faces of strangers, and this man, with his intense focus and quiet solitude, seemed a perfect subject.

As she sketched, she imagined the stories he might be writing or reading. Perhaps he was a poet, finding solace in the written word, or a historian lost in tales of the past. Her pen moved skillfully across the page, bringing his image to life with each stroke. She became so absorbed in her drawing that she almost didn't notice when he looked up at her.

Their eyes met, and **Veronica** felt a jolt, an unexpected and undeniable connection. She quickly looked away, her heart pounding. She continued drawing, hoping he hadn't noticed her staring.

Chris, the man with the book, had indeed noticed. He felt the weight of her gaze, and when their eyes met, he felt something stir within him, something he hadn't felt in a long time. His curiosity was piqued by the young woman who seemed so absorbed in her sketching, and he decided to approach her.

Chris: Excuse me, may I sit here?

Veronica: Of course.

Chris sat down and placed his book on the table.

Chris: I couldn't help but notice you were sketching. May I see it?

Veronica hesitated for a moment before turning her sketchbook towards him. His eyes widened slightly when he saw the drawing. It was a perfect likeness, capturing not only his features but something deeper, something intangible.

Chris: This is amazing. You have incredible talent.

Veronica blushed, tucking a strand of hair behind her ear.

Veronica: Thank you. I often sketch people I see, especially when they're... interesting.

Chris: Interesting, huh? I suppose that's better than being called boring.

Veronica: Well, you were very focused. What were you reading?

Chris looked at his book, a worn-out old novel.

Chris: Just an old favorite. I'm a writer, though I can't say that with much confidence lately. I've been struggling with a lack of inspiration.

Veronica: A writer! That's wonderful. What do you write about?

Chris: Love, loss, the usual existential crises. But lately, it's been hard to find the right words.

Veronica: I understand. Art, in any form, can be a challenging process.

Their conversation flowed naturally, as if they had known each other for years. They talked about art and literature, their dreams and fears, and in those moments, the storm outside seemed to fade away. **Chris** told **Veronica** about his childhood in a small village in southern France, where he first discovered his love for storytelling. **Veronica**, in turn, shared parts of her journey as an artist.

Veronica: Paris is a city that inspires creativity. Every corner holds a new story, every face a new character.

Chris: That's true. Sometimes, I feel like the city itself is alive, breathing its history and dreams, speaking to those willing to listen.

As the café began to empty and the night grew darker, **Chris** looked at his watch and sighed.

Chris: I should probably be going; it's getting late.
Veronica: Yes, of course. It was really lovely talking to you.

Chris: Would you like to meet here again? Same time tomorrow?

Veronica: I'd love that.

As **Chris** prepared to leave, **Veronica** called out to him.

Veronica: Could I ask you for something?

Chris: Of course.

Veronica: Do you have any of your writings with you that I could read?

Chris: Why?

Veronica: Just curious. Maybe I could find some new inspiration from it.

Chris pulled out a small notebook from his pocket.

Chris: Here you go. It's a collection of my short stories. Maybe you'll find some inspiration in them, just as I found inspiration in meeting you today.

Veronica took the notebook, her fingers brushing against his, feeling a spark of connection.

Veronica: Thank you, **Chris**. I can't wait to read them.

Chris gave her one last smile before stepping out into the rain, fading into the night. **Veronica** watched him go, a feeling of excitement and anticipation washing over her. She opened the notebook and began to read, her heart filled with the beauty of his words.

That night, as she lay in bed, **Veronica** couldn't stop thinking about **Chris** and their conversation. She felt a connection to him, a kindred spirit who understood her struggles and triumphs in the creative process. As she drifted off to sleep, she dreamed of their next meeting and the stories they would share.

The next day, with the rain still falling, **Veronica** found herself eagerly awaiting her meeting with **Chris**. She arrived at the café early, prepared her sketchbook, and waited. She waited for a long time, fearing **Chris** might not come. To ease her worry, she flipped through the pages of his notebook. Each story was a window into his soul, revealing his hopes, fears, and dreams.

When **Chris** arrived, soaked from the rain but with a smile on his face, **Veronica**'s heart leaped.

Chris: Sorry for the delay, **Veronica**.

Veronica: Don't worry about it. I hope it wasn't for something major.

Chris: No, just traffic.

Veronica: Good. Tell me, how are you today?

Chris: I'm doing well.

Chris and **Veronica** spent hours talking, laughing, and sharing their art, forgetting about the outside world. As the days passed, their relationship grew deeper, and they found themselves looking forward to their time together more than anything else.

As the weeks turned into months, the stormy weather gave way to sunny days, but **Chris** and **Veronica** continued to meet at the café, deepening their bond with each meeting. They became sources of inspiration for each other, and their art flourished in ways they hadn't imagined.

One afternoon, as they sat by the window, **Chris** took **Veronica**'s hand and looked into her eyes.

Chris: **Veronica**, you've brought so much light into my life. I don't know how I was living without you.
Veronica: **Chris**, I feel the same way. You've inspired me in ways I never thought possible.

And so, in the heart of Paris, the first spark of what might become an epic love story was ignited.

Chapter Two: Revealing Secrets

Days in Paris grew brighter as summer approached, but the café by the Seine retained its charm, becoming a sanctuary for **Veronica** and **Chris**. Their daily meetings turned into a beloved routine, a brief escape from the outside world. The more they talked, the more they revealed their stories to each other, finding comfort and inspiration in their shared experiences.

One particularly warm afternoon, with sunlight streaming through the café windows, **Veronica** and **Chris** sat at their usual table. **Veronica** was sketching a landscape, her brow furrowed in concentration, while **Chris** was jotting down notes in his worn notebook.

Chris, breaking the comfortable silence, called out to **Veronica**

Chris: **Veronica**.

Veronica: Yes?

Chris: I've been thinking a lot about what you said the other day. About how art can be both a refuge and a discovery.

Veronica: Yes, I've always believed that. Art has a way of revealing truths we may not even know we're hiding.

Chris: That's true. Writing has always been my way of dealing with my emotions, trying to make sense of the chaos inside.

Veronica: What is it you're trying to understand, **Chris**? I've noticed you seem lost in thought often, but I don't know why.

Chris hesitated for a moment.

Veronica: You don't have to tell me if you don't want to.

Chris: I've lost someone very dear to me. She was my lover, my muse, my everything.

Veronica: Where is she now?

Chris: She left without a trace, and since then, I've been lost.

Veronica: I'm so sorry, **Chris**. That must have been incredibly hard.

Chris: It was. But meeting you has been like a breath of fresh air. You've brought something into my life that I thought I'd lost forever.

Veronica: You've done the same for me, **Chris**. Your stories and passion have inspired me in ways I never thought possible.

Their conversation continued, each word weaving a deeper bond between them. They talked about their pasts, their hopes for the future, and the dreams they feared might never come true. **Chris** learned that **Veronica** had moved to Paris from a small town, hoping to immerse herself in the art world. She faced many challenges but remained determined to pursue her passion.

Veronica: Paris can be a tough place to make a name for yourself.

Chris: True. Every artist's journey is fraught with obstacles and challenges to bring their art to light.
Veronica: But every challenge I've faced has been an opportunity to grow, to push myself further.

Chris: You're stronger than you realize, **Veronica**. Your art reflects that strength.

As they continued to talk, **Veronica** couldn't help but notice how **Chris**'s eyes sparkled when he spoke about his writing. It was clear that his passion for storytelling ran deep, and she felt honored to be a part of his creative journey.

One evening, as the café began to empty and the sky turned a deep shade of pink, **Chris** pulled out a small, intricately designed box from his bag.

Chris: I've been working on something, and I wanted to share it with you.

Veronica: What is it, **Chris**?

Chris opened the box to reveal a delicate necklace, inside which was a small portrait of **Veronica** that he had sketched from memory. This gesture, filled with love and care, perfectly captured her essence and the profound connection they shared.

Chris: I know it's not much, but I wanted you to have this. A symbol of my appreciation for everything you've brought into my life.

Veronica's eyes filled with tears as she took the necklace.

Veronica: **Chris**, this is beautiful. Thank you so much.

She put on the necklace, feeling its weight against her heart. In that moment, she knew that their bond was something rare and precious, something that would endure despite the challenges ahead.

The next day, as they sat by the Seine, wrapped in each other's arms, they knew that their love would be tested in ways they could never have imagined. But they also knew that their bond was strong enough to withstand whatever the future held.

Their days continued, each one a precious gift as they cherished every moment together. **Veronica** and **Chris** found solace in their art, pouring their emotions into their creations. **Chris**'s writing took on a new depth, infused with the passion and pain of their shared journey. **Veronica**'s paintings also reflected their love and the bittersweet reality of their situation.

One evening, as the sun set over the Seine, casting a golden glow on the water, **Chris** and **Veronica** sat by the riverbank. **Veronica** brought her sketchbook, and **Chris** brought his notebook, finding comfort in the act of creating.

Veronica: Do you ever wonder how things would be different if we hadn't met?

Chris: Sometimes. But I try to focus on what we have now, instead of what might have been. All I know is that every moment with you is a treasure.

Veronica: You're right. We have to make the most of every moment we have.

Chris reached out and took her hand, his fingers intertwining with hers.

Chris: No matter what happens, **Veronica**, know that you've changed my life in ways I never thought possible. You've given me the strength to write again, to dream again.

Veronica: And you, **Chris**, have shown me what it means to truly follow your passion. For that, I will be forever grateful.

As the stars began to twinkle above, **Chris** read to **Veronica** from his latest story, his voice a soothing balm to her soul. They sat there, wrapped in each other's warmth, their hearts beating in unison. In that moment, they knew that their love was something beautiful and eternal.

Weeks passed, and they spent their days exploring the city, visiting art galleries and bookstores, finding joy in the little things. Every moment was a testament to their love, a reminder that even in the face of adversity, there was beauty to be found.

One afternoon, as they wandered through a flower market, **Veronica** stopped to admire a bouquet of roses. **Chris** noticed her fascination and bought the flowers, handing them to her with a smile.

Chris: For you, my love. A symbol of our enduring passion.

Veronica: They're perfect, **Chris**. Thank you.

That night, as they sat in **Veronica**'s studio, surrounded by her paintings and the scent of roses, they made a promise to each other. No matter what the future held, they would live each day to the fullest, cherishing every moment they had together.

Chapter Three: The Growth of Love

The summer sun cast a warm, golden glow over Paris, illuminating the city's streets and filling its residents with a renewed sense of energy and optimism. For **Veronica** and **Chris**, these days were like the brushstrokes of a skilled painter, each one adding depth and color to their love story. The bond between them grew stronger with each passing day, nourished by their shared passions and the quiet moments they spent together.

Their favorite café by the Seine had become a sanctuary, a place where they could escape the demands of the world and simply be with each other. On one particularly beautiful afternoon, the café was bustling with life, the clinking of cups and enthusiastic conversations forming a lively backdrop to their intimate world.

Veronica had brought her sketchbook, as usual, and was working on a new piece inspired by the café's vibrant energy. **Chris**, the ever-dedicated writer, was jotting down notes for a new story, his eyes occasionally drifting to **Veronica**, who seemed to embody inspiration itself.

Veronica: **Chris**, I've been thinking about your stories. I feel like I can see them in my mind when you describe them.

Chris: That's because you're an artist, **Veronica**. You see the world in a way most people don't. It's one of the things I love about you.

Veronica: Thank you, **Chris**. But I think your writing makes me feel like I'm part of something bigger, like our stories are intertwined.

Chris: They are intertwined, **Veronica**. You've become my muse, and I can't imagine my life without you.

Their connection deepened with every shared moment, each word and gesture a testament to their growing affection. They spent their days exploring Paris together, visiting art galleries and bookstores, finding inspiration in the city's rich history and culture. The streets of Paris became the backdrop to their love, each step a new chapter in their unfolding story.

One sunny afternoon, as they walked along the Seine, **Chris** suddenly stopped and turned to **Veronica**.

Chris: I have a surprise for you. **Veronica**: Oh? What kind of surprise?

Chris: Follow me.

Chris led her to a hidden courtyard filled with blooming flowers and the sweet scent of jasmine. In the center of the courtyard was a small, enchanting fountain, its waters sparkling in the sunlight.

Chris: This is one of my favorite places in Paris.

Veronica: It's magical, **Chris**. What is this place?

Chris: It's my secret place. I come here when I need to think, to find inspiration. And now, I want to share it with you.

They sat by the fountain, their fingers intertwined, and talked about their dreams and aspirations. **Chris** told **Veronica** about his desire to write a novel that captured the essence of their love, a story that would endure long after they were gone.

Chris: I want to write something that makes people believe in love again, something that reminds them that even in the face of adversity, love is worth fighting for.

Veronica: I believe you can do that, **Chris**. Your words have the power to touch people's hearts, to change their lives. And I'll be here, every step of the way, supporting you.

Their sessions in the courtyard became a cherished ritual, a time for them to connect and draw strength from each other. As the weeks passed, their love grew like the flowers around them, each day bringing them closer together.

One evening, as the sun set over Paris, casting a warm golden glow over the city, **Chris** and **Veronica** found themselves on a bridge overlooking the Seine. The water below shimmered with the reflection of the setting sun, creating a scene straight out of a fairy tale.

Chris: **Veronica**, there's something I need to tell you.

Veronica: What is it, **Chris**?

Chris: I know we've only known each other for a short time, but I feel like I've known you my entire life. You've brought so much joy and inspiration into my world, and I can't imagine my life without you.

Tears filled **Veronica**'s eyes as she listened to his words, her heart swelling with love.

Veronica: **Chris**, I feel the same way. You've shown me a love I never thought possible.

Chris: **Veronica**, I love you. I love you more than words can express.

Veronica: I love you too, **Chris**. With all my heart.

They embraced, their hearts beating as one, as the sun set behind them, casting a golden glow over their love. In that moment, they knew that no matter what challenges lay ahead, their love was strong enough to overcome them.

As they walked back to the café, hand in hand, they felt a sense of peace and contentment, knowing they had found something truly special in each other. Their love, like the city of Paris, was timeless and enduring, a beacon of hope in a world full of uncertainties.

Veronica and **Chris** continued to explore the city, finding new places that inspired their art and deepened their connection. They visited the Louvre, marveling at the masterpieces that had stood the test of time, and strolled through the gardens of Versailles, their love blooming amidst the beauty of the past.

Each moment they spent together was a testament to their love, a reminder that even in the face of adversity, love could flourish and thrive. They knew that their journey was just beginning, and that their love story would continue to unfold in ways they had never imagined.

And so, the love story of **Veronica** and **Chris** blossomed, a beautiful and enduring testament to the power of love and the magic of a chance encounter.

Chapter Four: Hidden Shadows

As summer gradually turned to autumn, the warm colors of the Parisian landscape began to change, casting the city in hues of gold, crimson, and amber. The vibrant energy of summer gave way to a more tranquil and reflective atmosphere, and with it came subtle shifts in **Veronica** and **Chris**'s world.

Their love had blossomed beautifully over the past months, but beneath the surface, **Veronica**'s health continued to decline. She tried to hide her suffering from **Chris**, not wanting to cast a shadow over the joy they had found in each other. However, the signs became harder to conceal with each passing day.

On a chilly morning, while they were strolling through the Tuileries Garden, **Veronica** felt a wave of fatigue wash over her. She slowed her pace, trying to catch her breath without alarming **Chris**.

Chris: Are you okay, **Veronica**?

Veronica: Just a little tired, that's all. I think I need to sit down for a bit.

They found a bench overlooking a tranquil pond, where ducks glided gracefully across the water's surface. **Chris** watched **Veronica** closely, his concern growing. He reached out and took her hand, his touch gentle and reassuring.

Chris: **Veronica**, you've looked pale lately, and you seem to tire easily. Are you sure you're, okay?

Veronica: There's something I need to tell you, **Chris**.

Chris: Of course, anything. Remember, we can face anything together.

Veronica: I've been diagnosed with a rare illness. It's been getting worse, and I didn't want to worry you, but I can't hide it from you any longer.

Chris: **Veronica**, what does this mean?

Veronica: It means I don't have much time left, **Chris**.

Chris: Why didn't you tell me earlier?

Veronica: I didn't want to burden you. The moments I've spent with you, **Chris**, have been some of the happiest of my life, and I didn't want to spoil them with my illness. I wanted our time together to be filled with joy, not worry.

Chris: No… there must be a solution.

Veronica: I wish there was, **Chris**. But unfortunately, fate has spoken.

Chris: We'll face this together, **Veronica**. You're not alone in this. I love you, and I'm not going anywhere.

Veronica felt a wave of comfort wash over her, knowing she no longer had to carry the burden of her secret alone. They sat in silence for a while, holding each other's hands as life continued around them.

As the days passed, **Chris** became more attentive, always by **Veronica**'s side, supporting her in every way he could. He accompanied her to doctor's appointments, helped her with daily tasks, and ensured she never felt alone. Their love, which had been a source of joy and inspiration, now became a source of strength and resilience.

On a rainy evening, as they sat in **Veronica**'s studio surrounded by her paintings, **Chris** picked up a paintbrush and started painting beside her. He wasn't an artist by nature, but he wanted to share in her world, to nurture her passion on a deeper level.

Veronica: **Chris**, you don't have to do this. You have your writing.

Chris: I want to experience what you experience, **Veronica**. I want to see the world through your eyes, even if just for a moment.

They painted together, their strokes intertwining and complementing each other, creating a masterpiece born from their shared love and determination. In those moments, their fears and worries seemed to melt away, leaving only the pure, unconditional joy of creation.

As the rain continued to pour outside, **Chris** and **Veronica**'s bond grew stronger. They found solace in their art, using it as a means to cope with the challenges they faced.

Veronica: **Chris**, you don't have to stay with me. You have your own life to live.

Chris: And what life is that without you, **Veronica**? You've become the air I breathe. How can anyone live without their breath?

Veronica: But, **Chris**…

Chris: I don't want to hear any more talk about this, **Veronica**. I'm here, and I'll always be here. Even if our time is short, we'll live it to the fullest.

Veronica: You're right. We should make the most of the time we have. I don't know how I would manage without you, **Chris**.

They sat in comfortable silence, the gentle sound of the fountain in the background. **Veronica**'s illness cast a shadow over their days, but it also deepened their appreciation for the time they spent together. They learned to find joy in the small moments and to cherish the simple pleasures life had to offer.

On one evening, as they walked along the Seine, the city lights reflecting on the water, **Chris** turned to **Veronica** with a determined look in his eyes.

Chris: **Veronica**, I have an idea. I want to document our journey, our love story. I want to write it all down so that our story lives on, no matter what happens.

Veronica: That sounds beautiful, **Chris**. I think it's a wonderful idea.

Chris: I'll start tomorrow. Every moment, every memory, will be written in my words. Our love will be immortalized, just like your paintings.

As the autumn leaves began to fall, **Veronica** and **Chris** continued to create, their love story unfolding like a masterpiece. They faced each challenge with courage and grace, drawing strength from their love and from each other.

The cold months set in, bringing with them more frequent hospital visits. **Chris** remained a constant presence, always ready with a comforting word or a gentle touch. They turned the small hospital room into a gallery of their shared creativity, **Veronica**'s paintings adorning the walls and **Chris**'s stories neatly arranged on the bedside table.

As the days grew shorter and the nights longer, **Chris** and **Veronica** continued to find strength in their love and in their art. Each new creation was a testament to their resilience, a reminder that even in the face of adversity, beauty could be found.

One evening, as they sat together by the window, watching the snow fall gently outside, **Chris** turned to **Veronica** with a tender smile.

Chris: Do you remember the first time we met? That rainy day at the café?

Veronica: Of course, I remember. It was the beginning of everything.

Chris: And do you remember what you said to me that day?

Veronica: I said that art has a way of revealing truths we may not even know we're hiding.

Chris: And you were right, **Veronica**. Our love has revealed many truths and many beautiful moments. And no matter what happens, those moments will last forever.

Chapter Five: The Announcement

Winter winds howled through the streets of Paris, carrying with them a chill that penetrated to the bone. The city, covered in a layer of snow, looked like a scene from a fairy tale, with twinkling lights at every corner. Despite the cold, the warmth of love between **Veronica** and **Chris** continued to grow, illuminating the darkest days of winter.

One evening, as the snow gently fell outside, **Veronica** and **Chris** found themselves in their favorite café by the Seine. The café was a haven from the cold, warm and lit with a soft glow that provided a comforting contrast to the icy streets outside. **Veronica** brought her sketchbook, and **Chris**, as usual, had his notebook.

Veronica: **Chris**, I've been thinking about our journey together. How far we've come and how much our love has grown.

Chris: It's been a wonderful journey, **Veronica**. I couldn't have made it without you, especially after my lover left me. If it weren't for you, I couldn't have continued.

Veronica: No, **Chris**. You've been my rock. Your love gave me strength when I needed it most. Your presence by my side helps me fight my illness.

Chris found himself at a moment he'd been waiting for, to present **Veronica** with a big surprise. He reached across the table and took her hand, his touch warm and reassuring.

Chris: And you, **Veronica**, have been my inspiration. You've brought so much light into my life, and I can't imagine a future without you.

Their eyes met, and in that moment, the world seemed to fade away, leaving only the two of them and the love they shared. **Chris** knew he couldn't wait any longer to express the depth of his feelings. He had been carrying a small, intricately designed box for weeks, waiting for the perfect moment to reveal it.

Chris: **Veronica**, there's something I want to tell you.

Veronica: What is it, **Chris**?

Taking a deep breath and gathering his courage, **Chris** opened the box to reveal a delicate ring adorned with a small, sparkling diamond.

Chris: **Veronica**, I love you more than words can express. You are my muse, my anchor, my everything. Will you marry me?

Veronica's eyes filled with sorrow.

Veronica: No, **Chris**, I can't do that. I can't condemn you to marry me, and I can't guarantee what your future with me will be like because of my illness.

Chris: This is my life, and I choose how I want to live it. I want to spend every moment, every second with you, even if it's only for a short time.

Veronica: Why are you doing this, **Chris**? You could go, leave me, and live your life with someone else. Believe me, I would understand and not blame you. What would hurt me more is seeing you watch me suffer.

Chris: Because you are my light, **Veronica**. Without you, there is no morning, no life, no breath to breathe. So, Miss **Veronica**, you haven't answered. Will you be my wife?

Tears filled **Veronica**'s eyes as she looked at the ring, her heart overflowing with love and joy.

Veronica: And I, **Chris**, love you so much. With all my heart, I say yes, I will marry you.

Chris's face lit up with a bright smile as he placed the ring on **Veronica**'s finger. They embraced, their hearts beating in harmony, while the café erupted in applause from other patrons who had witnessed the heartfelt proposal.

One evening, as they sat by the fireplace in **Chris**'s apartment, sipping hot chocolate and watching the flames dance, **Veronica** turned to **Chris** with a tender look.

Veronica: **Chris**, do you ever think about what it means to love someone unconditionally? To give your heart and soul to another person?

Chris: I think about it every day, **Veronica**. Your love has shown me what it means to be selfless, to put someone else's needs above your own. It's a powerful and transformative experience.

Veronica: I feel the same way, **Chris**. Our love has taught me so much about resilience and hope, about finding beauty amidst pain.

As they sat together, wrapped in each other's warmth, they knew their love was something rare and precious, a bond that would endure despite the challenges they faced. They found in each other a source of strength and inspiration, a love that would carry them through the darkest times.

The days grew longer, and the harshness of winter began to give way to the promise of spring. With the changing seasons came a renewed sense of hope and possibility. **Veronica** and **Chris** continued to create, their art a testament to their love and the journey they had undertaken together.

On a sunny afternoon, as they walked hand in hand through the Luxembourg Gardens, **Veronica** felt a sense of peace and contentment wash over her. The gardens were in full bloom, the vibrant colors and fragrant scents filling the air with a sense of renewal and rebirth.

Veronica: **Chris**, I want to spend every moment of my life with you. I want to create a future together, filled with love, art, and joy. I don't want to die, **Chris**. I want to live a full life with you.

Chris: And I want the same thing, **Veronica**. Our love is the foundation on which we will build our future. No matter what challenges we face, we will overcome them together. No illness will stop us from feeling joy and living every moment of love between us.

As they continued their walk through the garden, their hearts filled with hope and promise, they knew their love story was only just beginning. They had faced many trials and tribulations, but through it all, their love had remained steadfast and true.

Chapter Six: Moments of Happiness

As spring blossomed in Paris, the city came alive with colors and light, mirroring the blooming love between **Veronica** and **Chris**. The air was filled with the sweet scent of flowers, and the days grew longer, granting them more time to appreciate each other's presence. They embraced every moment, finding joy in the simplest pleasures and creating memories that would last a lifetime.

On a sunny afternoon, as they strolled hand in hand through the bustling streets of Montmartre, they were drawn into a small art gallery. The gallery showcased a collection of works by local artists, and **Veronica**'s eyes lit up at the sight of the vibrant paintings adorning the walls.

Veronica: **Chris**, look at these! They're amazing! The colors, the emotions—they're so powerful.

Chris: They really are. It's incredible how art can capture the essence of the human experience, isn't it?

Veronica: Absolutely. Each piece tells a story, a glimpse into the artist's soul.

They spent hours in the gallery, immersed in the beauty and creativity surrounding them. **Veronica**'s mind buzzed with inspiration, eager to return to her studio and start working on her own pieces. **Chris**, too, felt a renewed sense of purpose, his heart brimming with ideas for his next novel.

As they left the gallery, the sun began to set, casting a warm golden glow over the city. They walked along the Seine, the water reflecting the colors of the sky, and found a quiet spot to sit and watch the world go by.

Veronica: I'm so grateful for these moments we share. They mean everything to me.

Chris: Me too, **Veronica**. Every day with you is a gift, and I cherish every second.

Their love grew with each passing day, their connection deepening in ways they had never imagined. They explored the city together, discovering new places and weaving a tapestry of memories that bound their lives together. From picnics in the Jardin des Plantes to nighttime strolls along the Champs-Élysées, they found joy in the simplest moments.

One evening, as they sat on a bench overlooking the Eiffel Tower, **Chris** pulled a small leather-bound notebook from his bag.

Chris: **Veronica**, I've been working on something for you.

Veronica: What is it, **Chris**?

He handed her the notebook, his fingers brushing against hers.

Chris: It's a collection of poems I've written about us. About our love, our journey, and the moments we've shared.

Veronica's heart swelled with emotion as she opened the notebook and began to read. Each poem was a testament to their love, capturing the beauty and depth of their connection. Her eyes filled with tears as she read **Chris**'s heartfelt words, her soul touched by the honesty and passion behind each verse.

Veronica: **Chris**, this is beautiful. I don't know what to say. Thank you.

Chris: You don't need to say anything, **Veronica**. Just knowing you feel the same way is enough for me.

They sat together, wrapped in each other's warmth, as the city lights began to twinkle around them. In that moment, they felt an unbreakable bond, a love that transcended time and space.

As the weeks turned into months, **Veronica** and **Chris** continued to create, their art blossoming in ways they had never imagined. **Chris**'s writings took on new dimensions, filled with the emotion and inspiration he drew from **Veronica**. Her paintings, too, reflected their love, each brushstroke a testament to the joy and beauty they found in each other.

One sunny afternoon, as they worked side by side in **Veronica**'s studio, **Chris** looked at her with a thoughtful expression.

Chris: **Veronica**, I've been thinking about our future. About the life we want to build together.

Veronica: What do you mean, **Chris**?

Chris: I want us to live our dreams, **Veronica**. To create a life filled with love, art, and adventure. I want us to travel the world, to see new places and experience new things. And most importantly, I want us to do it together.

Veronica: **Chris**, that sounds wonderful. I want that too. I want to see the world with you, to create memories that will last a lifetime. But sometimes, what we want isn't always possible.

Chris: Why do you say that, **Veronica**?

Veronica: We can't keep lying to ourselves, **Chris**. No matter how much we dream and hope for the future, the end remains the same for us.

Chris: Please, stop saying that. Every time you say that, **Veronica**, it breaks my heart. I know that my love for you isn't enough to change fate.

Veronica: And what can I do, **Chris**? Every time I see you so hopeful and dreaming, I fear for the time when I have to leave you. It will be so hard for you.

Chris: Don't worry about me, **Veronica**. All I want now is for us to achieve the greatest amount of happiness together, no matter the circumstances.

Veronica: And how do you propose we do that?

Chris: What do you want to do, **Veronica**, in the rest of your life? What did you dream of doing before the shadow of illness ruined everything for you?

Veronica: I always wished to sit with my lover in a boat floating down the Seine, and I always wanted to climb the Eiffel Tower.

Chris: You mean you've never climbed the Eiffel Tower?

Veronica: No, I've always been afraid of heights, so I never got the chance.

Chris: What else?

Veronica: Watching a small concert with my lover and seeing the famous paintings in every museum.

Chris smiled; his heart filled with hope.

Chris: Then let's do it, **Veronica**. Let's make our dreams a reality.

As they continued to work, their hearts full of promise, they knew their love was something rare and beautiful, a bond that would withstand any challenges ahead.

One evening, as they sat by the Seine watching the boats pass by, **Veronica** turned to **Chris** with a smile.

Veronica: Do you remember the night we first met?

Chris: How could I forget? It was the beginning of everything. **Veronica**: I knew from that moment that you were someone special, **Chris**. Someone who would change my life in ways I could never have imagined.

Chris: And you've changed my life, **Veronica**. You've brought so much light and love into my world. I can't imagine a future without you.

As the stars began to twinkle above them, they knew their love was a guiding light, a beacon that would lead them through the darkest times. They sat together, wrapped in each other's warmth, their hearts beating in harmony.

With each passing day, **Veronica** and **Chris**'s love grew stronger. They faced the challenges of **Veronica**'s illness with courage and grace, finding solace in their art and in each other. Their love became a source of strength, a reminder that even in the face of adversity, beauty could be found.

One afternoon, as they worked in their studio, **Veronica** looked at **Chris** with a thoughtful expression.

Veronica: **Chris**, I want to create something that will last forever. Something that captures the essence of our love.

Chris: What do you have in mind, **Veronica**?

Veronica: A series of paintings and stories inspired by our journey together. A legacy of love that will live on after we're gone.

Chris: That sounds beautiful, **Veronica**. Let's do it. Let's create something that will endure.

As they began work on their project, their hearts filled with hope and promise, they knew their love was something truly special. They found in each other a source of inspiration and strength, a bond that would withstand any challenges ahead.

And so, **Veronica** and **Chris**'s love continued to flourish, a beautiful and enduring testament to the power of love and the magic of a chance encounter.

Chapter Seven: A Beautiful Night

As the autumn leaves turned to radiant shades of gold and red, the air was filled with a sense of urgency. **Veronica** and **Chris** spent their days finding solace in each other's presence, knowing their time together was precious. The reality of **Veronica**'s illness cast a shadow over their moments of happiness, but they remained determined to make the most of their time together.

One chilly evening, as they sat on a bench overlooking the Seine, **Chris** noticed **Veronica**'s gaze fixed on the Eiffel Tower. It stood tall and majestic against the evening sky, illuminated by thousands of twinkling lights.

Chris: **Veronica**, would you like to go up?

Veronica: Now?

Chris: It has been one of your wishes, hasn't it?

Veronica: Yes, but...

Chris: But what? There is no need to be afraid, **Veronica**. I'll be with you.

Veronica smiled, her eyes reflecting the lights of the tower.

Veronica: I'd love that, **Chris**. It sounds like the perfect way to capture this moment.

Hand in hand, they made their way to the Eiffel Tower. The climb was slow and deliberate, with **Chris** supporting **Veronica** every step of the way. When they reached the top, they were greeted by a breathtaking view of Paris, the city they both loved deeply.

Veronica: This is beautiful. I feel like we're on top of the world. **Chris**: We are, **Veronica**. We're on top of our world, and nothing can take this moment from us.

They stood there, taking in the panoramic view of the city below. The twinkling lights, the bustling streets, and the gentle flow of the Seine all seemed to merge into a symphony of life and love. In that moment, they felt a deep sense of peace and connection, knowing their love was strong enough to overcome any challenge.

As the night grew darker, they descended from the tower and made their way to a nearby café. The warmth of the café embraced them, and they found a cozy corner to sit and talk. **Chris** reached into his bag and pulled out a small, wrapped gift.

Chris: **Veronica**, I have something for you.

Veronica: **Chris**, you didn't have to get me anything.

Chris: Just open it.

Veronica unwrapped the gift to reveal an exquisitely crafted journal. The cover was adorned with intricate designs, and her name was engraved in gold letters. She opened the journal to find that **Chris** had filled the pages with his thoughts, memories, and poems about their time together.

Veronica: **Chris**, this is amazing. You've captured everything perfectly. Thank you.

Chris: I wanted to create something that would last forever, **Veronica**. A testament to our love and the journey we've shared.

Tears filled **Veronica**'s eyes as she leaned in to kiss him.

Veronica: I love you, **Chris**. With all my heart.

They spent the rest of the evening reminiscing about their adventures, their love, and the dreams they had for the future. As they talked, they knew that no matter what the future held, their bond would remain unbreakable.

The following days were filled with moments of tenderness and reflection. **Veronica**'s condition continued to deteriorate, but she faced each day with courage and grace, drawing strength from **Chris**'s unwavering support. They visited their favorite places in the city, finding comfort in the familiar sights and sounds of Paris.

One day, as they strolled through the Luxembourg Gardens, **Veronica** paused to admire the vibrant flowers.

Veronica: **Chris**, I've always loved this place. It feels like a sanctuary of beauty and tranquility.

Chris: It is a special place, **Veronica**. Just like you.

Veronica: Promise me, **Chris**, that no matter what happens, you'll always remember the good times we've had. The love we've shared.

Chris: I promise, **Veronica**. Our love will always be a part of me. It will live on through our art, our memories, and the people whose lives we've touched.

As the days grew colder, **Veronica** and **Chris** found solace in their creative pursuits. They painted, wrote, and poured their emotions into their work, creating a legacy of love that would endure beyond their lifetimes.

One evening, as they sat by the fireplace in **Chris**'s apartment, **Veronica** looked at him with a smile.

Veronica: **Chris**, do you remember the first time we met?

Chris: Of course, I remember. It was in that little café by the Seine. You were sketching, and I couldn't take my eyes off you.

Veronica: And I remember thinking how handsome you were, so focused on your book. It's funny how life brings people together in unexpected ways.

Chris: I'm grateful for every moment we've shared, **Veronica**. You've changed my life in ways I never imagined.

As the fire crackled and the night grew darker, they sat in comfortable silence, their hearts beating in harmony. They knew their love was a guiding light, a beacon that would lead them through the darkest times.

Chapter Eight: The Final Days

As the crisp air turned colder with the advancing season in Paris, every day for **Veronica** and **Chris** was a mix of happiness and sorrow. The awareness of **Veronica**'s deteriorating health cast a shadow over their joyful moments, but they remained determined to enjoy every precious moment they had left together.

On a cold day, they decided to visit a museum featuring Monet's stunning Water Lilies paintings. The serene and peaceful environment of the museum provided a sanctuary from the outside world. As they walked through the gallery, holding hands, **Veronica**'s eyes wandered over the magnificent paintings.

Veronica: **Chris**, look how Monet captured the light and reflections. It's like stepping into a dream.

Chris: It's beautiful, **Veronica**. Just like your art.

They spent hours exploring the museum, drawing inspiration from the masterpieces surrounding them. For **Veronica**, every moment felt like a gift, an opportunity to experience the beauty of life and art with the man she loved.

As the days grew colder, **Veronica** and **Chris** found themselves spending more time inside their cozy apartment. They continued to create, their art a testament to their love and resilience. **Chris**'s writings flourished, filled with the emotion and inspiration he drew from **Veronica**. Her paintings, too, reflected the depth of their connection, each brushstroke a tribute to their shared journey.

One evening, as they sat by the fireplace, **Veronica** turned to **Chris** with a wistful look.

Veronica: **Chris**, have you ever wondered how things would be if they were different? If I were healthy?

Chris: Of course, I've dreamed of a full life with you. A home for just the two of us, away from the world. Perhaps a child would visit us in a couple of years, and we'd spend the rest of our lives together. It saddens me deeply, **Veronica**, but I've learned to focus on the present and appreciate the moments we have. Our love is stronger than any illness.

Veronica: You're right, **Chris**. Our love is a gift, and I wouldn't trade it for anything.

As the fire crackled and the night grew darker, they sat in comfortable silence, their hearts beating in harmony. They knew their time together was limited, but they were determined to make the most of every moment.

The following days were filled with moments of tenderness and reflection. **Chris** took **Veronica** to their favorite places in the city, from the bustling streets of Montmartre to the tranquil beauty of the Jardin des Plantes. They found joy in the simplest pleasures, like sharing a warm croissant at their favorite bakery or watching the sunset over the Seine.

On one unforgettable evening, they attended a small concert in an enchanting old theater in Le Marais. The music, a blend of classical and contemporary pieces, filled the atmosphere with magic. **Veronica** rested her head on **Chris**'s shoulder, feeling the warmth of his embrace.

Veronica: **Chris**, this is perfect. I wish this moment could last forever.

Chris: In a way, it will, **Veronica**. As long as we remember it, this moment will always be with us.

The music continued, and they swayed together, lost in the enchantment of the night. In those moments, they felt invincible, their love a shield against the world's hardships.

Veronica's condition continued to worsen, but she faced each day with courage and grace. **Chris** remained by her side, his unwavering support a source of strength and comfort.

One day, as they sat in their favorite café, **Chris** pulled a manuscript from his bag.

Chris: **Veronica**, I've finished writing our story.
Veronica: Really? Can I read it?

Chris: Of course. It's all there—every moment, every memory.

Veronica took the manuscript, her fingers trembling as she began to read. Tears filled her eyes as she saw their journey captured in **Chris**'s beautiful prose. Each page was a labor of love, a testament to the bond they shared.

Veronica: **Chris**, this is amazing. You've captured everything perfectly.

Chris: I wanted to make sure our love would live on, no matter what happens.

Veronica: Thank you, **Chris**. This means more to me than you can imagine.

She leaned in to kiss him, her heart full of love and gratitude. Then, **Veronica** coughed heavily, which sent a pang of fear through **Chris**'s heart.

Chris: **Veronica**, are you okay?

Veronica: I'm always okay when you're with me. Don't worry, I still have some time.

Chris took her hand, his voice full of emotion.

Chris: And you've changed my life, **Veronica**. You've brought so much light and love into my world. I can't imagine a future without you.

As the stars began to twinkle above them, they knew their love was a guiding light, a beacon that would lead them through the darkest times. They sat together, wrapped in each other's warmth, their hearts beating in unison.

Chapter Nine: The Last Night

As winter settled over Paris, the city turned into a magical wonderland, with twinkling lights and a blanket of snow covering the streets. For **Veronica** and **Chris**, the days grew shorter and more precious, every moment together a treasured memory.

One evening, as the first snowflakes began to fall, **Veronica** and **Chris** decided to spend a special night together. They wanted to make it unforgettable, a testament to their love that would endure through time. **Veronica** lay on the bed due to her deteriorating condition, but she didn't want her last moments to be spent in bed. She wanted to make it a lasting memory and spoke to **Chris**, who was sitting beside her, saddened by her condition.

Veronica: **Chris**, are you here, my love?

Chris: I'm here. Don't worry, always by your side.

Veronica: I want to go outside. I don't want my last moments to be on the bed.

Chris: But your condition is very bad, **Veronica**. You can't go out like this.

Veronica: I can, as long as you're with me, my strength in life.

Chris felt a pang of sadness, his eyes welling up slightly, but he didn't show it to her.

Chris: Where do you want to go, **Veronica**?

Veronica: Let's go to the Eiffel Tower. It feels like the perfect place for our last night.

Chris: Look at you, little adventurer. You're not afraid of the Eiffel Tower anymore.

Veronica: It's all because of you, **Chris**. Your love gave me the strength to face my fears. And now, things are different. Why should I fear anything when my end is near?

Chris felt sorrowful.

Chris: Please don't say that. I can't believe this. What will I do without you...?

Veronica: **Chris**, my love, I hate seeing you so sad. This is not what we agreed upon. Do you remember our agreement?

Chris: Of course, to not focus on the illness and to live every moment to the fullest.

Veronica: Then let's go and live the moment.

Chris, his heart swelling with love.

Chris: Sure, **Veronica**. Let's go make it an unforgettable night.

They wrapped up in warm coats and scarves, their breaths visible in the cold air as they headed to the magical spot. The Eiffel Tower stood tall and majestic against the night sky, illuminated by thousands of twinkling lights. It was a sight that never failed to take their breath away.

At the base of the tower, **Chris** took **Veronica**'s hand, his touch warm and reassuring.

Chris: Are you ready, my love?

Veronica: I'm ready, **Chris**. Let's do this.

They took the elevator to the top of the tower, the anticipation building with each passing moment. When they finally stepped onto the observation deck, they were greeted by a breathtaking view of the city below. The lights of Paris stretched out before them, creating a sea of shimmering beauty.

Veronica: This is incredible. The view makes me feel like we're on top of the world.

Chris: We are, **Veronica**. We're on top of our world, and nothing can take this moment from us.

They stood in silence, taking in the panoramic view of the city they loved so much. The twinkling lights, the bustling streets, the gentle flow of the Seine—all seemed to merge into a symphony of life and love. In that moment, they felt a deep sense of peace and connection, knowing their love was strong enough to overcome any challenge.

This was the defining moment. **Veronica** felt severely weak, her strength fading away bit by bit until she nearly collapsed, but **Chris** caught her in his arms.

Veronica: So, this is it, isn't it?

Chris: No, **Veronica**, this can't be it. Please don't leave me.

Veronica: It saddens me, **Chris**. Not death, but leaving you behind. I never wanted to do this.

Chris: No, **Veronica**, you won't go anywhere. Remember, our love is strong enough to face anything.

Veronica: I remember seeing you for the first time, **Chris**, as if it was yesterday. You were that handsome young man sitting in the corner.

Chris: And you, **Veronica**, were the artist sitting across from me.

Veronica: I wished time had stood still on that day so this moment wouldn't come, **Chris**.

Chris: **Veronica**, please don't go. **Veronica**: I see it now, **Chris**.

Chris: What do you see?

Veronica: The light. It's so beautiful, **Chris**.

Chris: No, **Veronica**, don't go. Stay with me.

Veronica: That's what I've always wished for, with all my heart. Goodbye, **Chris**.

Veronica passed away in **Chris**'s arms at the top of the Eiffel Tower. **Chris** held **Veronica** tightly in his arms, crying out in pain from the loss. His cry was so loud and powerful that he thought everyone in

Paris could hear it. That was the last moment of their epic story, but perhaps fate had another plan for them.

Chapter Ten: Revelation

As winter tightened its grip on Paris, **Chris** found himself spending more time alone, lost in thought. Memories of **Veronica**—her smile, her laughter, her unwavering love—became a source of comfort and solace. Yet, as the days grew colder, a sense of unease began to creep into his mind.

One evening, as **Chris** sat in his favorite café by the Seine, he opened the journal he had given to **Veronica**. The pages were filled with his thoughts and memories, but as he read them, he felt that something was off. He couldn't shake the feeling that something was missing, a piece of the puzzle he had overlooked.

A sudden snap back to reality occurred when the **waiter** came to take his order.

Waiter: Hello, sir. What would you like to order?

Chris: I'd like some coffee.

Waiter: Shall I bring you a latte as well, as usual?

Chris: What do you mean by that?

Waiter: I mean, you always come here and order coffee and a latte together. Did I make a mistake?

Chris: Wasn't there someone with me?

Waiter: I'm sorry, sir. I didn't mean to cause any trouble.

Chris: Answer me.

Waiter: Yes, sir, you always came alone.

Chris: You never saw a lady with me here?

Waiter: No, sir, you always came alone.

Chris was shocked. He decided to take a walk along the Seine, hoping the fresh air would clear his mind. The city was quiet, the snow muffling the sounds of traffic and footsteps. As he walked, his thoughts turned inward, and he began to question the reality of his memories.

Chris: **Veronica**, why do I feel like you're slipping away from me?

As **Chris** continued walking, his mind drifted to the day he first met **Veronica**. He remembered the café, the sketchbook, the way she had captivated him completely. But as he replayed the scene in his mind, he realized there were inconsistencies, details that didn't quite add up.

Chris's heart raced as he pieced together fragments of his memories. He returned to his apartment and pulled out the manuscript he had written, his hands trembling as he flipped through the pages. As he read the story, the truth began to unfold before his eyes.

Veronica wasn't real. She had never existed. She was a figment of **Chris**'s imagination, a reflection of the woman he had loved and lost. The illness, the love story, the adventures they had shared—all were creations of his mind, a way to cope with the pain of his lover's departure.

Chris's lover had left him suddenly, and he had never fully understood why. In his grief and confusion, he created **Veronica** as a way to make sense of her absence. **Veronica**'s illness was a convenient explanation, a reason that made sense amidst his broken heart.

As the truth settled over him, **Chris** felt a wave of emotions—shock, sorrow, and a strange sense of relief. He realized that his mind had crafted **Veronica** as a means of healing, to process the pain and find solace in his loneliness. Then, **Veronica** appeared before him in his imagination.

Chris: So, you weren't real, just a mirage.

Veronica: Who decides what is real and what is a mirage? I was real when you needed me, **Chris**. You created me so you could heal from your heartbreak. When my task was complete, I returned to my natural state, a mere mirage.

Chris: Then why did my lover leave me? Where did I go wrong?

Veronica: If I could answer that question, **Chris**, I would. But I only know what you know and can't know what you don't.

Chris: What should I do now?

Veronica: Do what you do best, **Chris**. Write and imagine.

Then, **Veronica** vanished. **Chris** sat at his desk; his heart heavy with the weight of his revelation. He picked up his pen and began to write, his thoughts pouring onto the page. He wrote about his lover, the love they had shared, and the heartbreak he had endured. He wrote about **Veronica**, the imaginary woman who had helped him navigate his grief.

Through his writing, **Chris** found a way to make sense of his emotions. He poured his heart into the pages, creating a narrative that honored both his real love and the imaginary one he had invented. He realized that **Veronica**, though not real, had served a vital purpose in his life. She had been a bridge between his past and his future, helping him heal and move forward.

As **Chris** finished his writing, he felt a sense of peace wash over him. He knew his journey was far from over, but he also knew he had the strength to face whatever lay ahead. He had found a way to honor his past while embracing the possibilities of the future.

In the heart of Paris, under the watchful gaze of the Eiffel Tower and the gentle flow of the Seine, **Chris**'s love continued to flourish—both the love he had lost and the love he had imagined. His story, though rooted in heartbreak, was a testament to the resilience of the human spirit and the power of imagination.

As **Chris** walked along the Seine, memories of his time with **Veronica** filled his heart with warmth. He knew she had been a creation of his mind, but she had also been a source of strength and inspiration. He found joy in simple pleasures, like watching the sunset over the river or listening to the laughter of children playing in the park.

One evening, as the sun set over Paris, casting a warm golden glow over the city, **Chris** stood on the bridge where he often imagined being with **Veronica**. He closed his eyes, felt the gentle breeze on his face, and whispered a silent thank you to the woman who had been both real and imagined, for the love and lessons she had brought into his life.

In that moment, **Chris** felt a deep sense of peace and connection. He knew that his love, both real and imagined, was eternal—a beacon of light that would carry him through the rest of his life. And as he continued his journey, he carried the memories of both loves with him, finding beauty and inspiration in every step.

Chris's legacy of love endured, a testament to the power of love, imagination, and the resilience of the human spirit. His story, captured in words and art, touched the hearts of people around the world, reminding them that even in the face of adversity, love can thrive and endure.

In the heart of Paris, under the watchful gaze of the Eiffel Tower and the gentle flow of the Seine, the echoes of **Chris**'s eternal love—both real and imagined—continued to resonate, a beautiful and enduring tribute to the magic of a chance encounter and the transformative power of love.

The End